Meet Duffy T. McGraw

Will You Be My Friend?

Virginia Giordano

Illustrated by Lisa Brennan

ISBN: 1530840600
ISBN 13: 9781530840601
Library of Congress Control Number: 2016905786
CreateSpace, Charleston, SC
Available from Amazon.com, CreateSpace.com, and other retail outlets

To Mike, Tug, Mickey, Robbie, Marco, and, of course, Duffy—

loving teachers and companions to all who were fortunate to cross their paths

Duffy and his family have moved into their new home. As they unpack, Duffy goes for a walk and sees a bird sitting on the branch of a tree.

"Hello, bird. I have just moved here. Do you want to be my friend?"

"No, I have feathers, and you have fur. We are very different."

"Why does that matter?" Duffy asks.

"I don't know, but I was told that it does," the bird says.

"What do you like to do?" Duffy asks.

"I like to sing. Chirp, chirp, chirp!"

Duffy dances as he hears the sounds and says, *"I love singing too. Bow-wow-wow! See, we are alike. We can be friends. Come over to my house, and we can play."*

The bird looks at Duffy and says, *"I have to look for worms now. I'm hungry. I'll come to your house later."*

Duffy continues his walk and sees a cat in the front yard of a big green house.

"*Hello, cat,*" Duffy says. "*I just moved here. Do you want to be my friend?*"

The cat looks at Duffy. "*Don't you know that I'm a cat? Cats and dogs do not like each other.*"

"*No, I didn't know that,*" Duffy says. "*Who told you?*"

"*Everyone!*" says the cat.

"*Really?*" Duffy asks. "*I don't believe that. I see you like to play with a ball, and so do I. I have a big red ball. See, we are alike. We can be friends. Come over to my house later, and we can play.*"

"*Will you have a bowl of milk for me if I get thirsty?*" asks the cat.

"*Of course! You are my friend. See you later.*"

Duffy continues his walk.

Out of the corner of his eye, he sees a snake sliding along the ground under some big bushes. "*Good morning, snake. I just moved here. Do you want to be my friend?*"

The snake looks surprised and says, "*You want to be my friend? No one wants to be friends with snakes. Everyone seems afraid of us. People say that we are ugly and scare them.*"

Duffy says, "*I want to be your friend. I think that you are very beautiful. I see that you like to wiggle along the ground. Me too! Sometimes when I get excited, I wiggle. See, we are alike. We can be friends. Come over to my house later. We have a big yard with many bushes.*"

"*Will I make everyone afraid if they see me?*" the snake asks.

"*Of course not,*" Duffy says. "*You are my friend. See you later.*"

Duffy has walked far, and he is tired. So he decides to rest in the shade of a big tree.

He sees a group of tiny black ants running here and there. "Hello, ant," he says to one of them. "I just moved here. Do you want to be my friend?"

The ant does not stop working but shouts, "No, I do not have the time. I have to keep working."

Duffy says, "I can help you so that you can get your work done faster. Then we can play. I like to be busy too."

The ant stops and looks up at Duffy. "You would help *me* with my work?"

"Well, of course; friends should always help each other," Duffy says.

"Okay!" says the ant.

Duffy helps the ant move some leaves. "*See, we are alike. We can be friends.*"

When the work is almost done, Duffy says, "*Come over to my house later, and play in the garden. You have worked enough today.*"

Duffy continues to walk but stops when he hears loud noises. He turns his head to the left and sees a group of wild turkeys coming out of the woods.

Duffy runs up to them and shouts, "*Hello, turkeys. I just moved here. Will you be my friends?*"

The turkeys look at one another and laugh. The biggest turkey says, "*A dog wants to be friends with turkeys? That's silly. We are not alike. We are wild and make lots of noise.*"

Duffy says, "*Oh, yes, we are alike. I love to make noise when I see the mail carrier. Ruff, ruff, ruff. See, we can be friends. We are alike. Come over to my house later, and we can all play together.*"

As Duffy continues to walk, he sees a big field with horses. Some of the horses are eating hay, and some are running around. Duffy stops and calls out to them. *"Hello, horses. I just moved here. Do you want to be my friends?"*

One of the horses stops, walks over to the fence, and looks down at the little pug.

"Horses and dogs can't be friends. We are very big and strong, and you are small. We like to run and jump," she says.

"I love to run and jump too," Duffy says. He starts to run around and around. When he stops, he says, "See, we are alike. We can be friends. Come over to my house later, and we can run in the yard."

Duffy continues his walk, but before he gets too far, he sees a tiny gray mouse chewing on a piece of wood. Duffy stops and says, *"Hello, mouse. I just moved here. Do you want to be my friend?"*

The mouse stops chewing, looks at Duffy, and laughs. *"Why would a mouse and a dog be friends?"*

"Why wouldn't we be friends?" Duffy says. *"I see that you like to chew things. Me too! I like to chew shoes and balls. See, we are alike. We can be friends. Come over to my house later, and I will share some of my toys with you."*

Duffy walks on and spots a man coming out of a barn. He is carrying a bucket filled with corn. Duffy watches as the man empties the corn into a trough and walks away. All of a sudden, Duffy hears a noise and sees four pigs running to the corn and eating it. Duffy calls out to them.

"Hello, pigs. I just moved here. Do you want to be my friends?"

A pig looks up from his meal and says, *"Don't you see that we're eating? Don't bother us."*

Duffy says, *"I love to eat too. I don't like anyone to stop me when I'm eating either. See, we are alike. We can be friends. Come over to my house later, and I will share a snack with you."*

Duffy has walked a long way. He thinks it is now time to go home.

As he turns around, he sees a tiny lizard sunning herself on a rock by the side of the road. He stops and calls out to her. *"Hello, lizard. I just moved here. Do you want to be my friend?"*

The lizard looks up and says, "*Go away. I'm afraid of dogs.*"

"*Why?*" Duffy asks.

"*Because we are so different,*" the lizard says.

Duffy sighs.

"*We are not different. I like to take a nap every day in the sun too. It feels so good. See, we are alike. We can be friends. Come over to my house later, and you can rest in the sun in my front yard.*"

Duffy is tired and walks slowly back to his house.

As he approaches his gate he hears the sounds of a celebration!

When he opens the gate, he sees all his new friends playing, napping, eating, and resting in his yard.

Duffy smiles. He greets them one by one.

"Hello, my friend the bird."

"Hello, my friend the cat."

"Hello, my friend the snake."

"Hello, my friend the ant."

"Hello, my friend the wild turkey."

"Hello, my friend the horse."

"Hello, my friend the mouse."

"Hello, my friend the pig."

"Hello, my friend the lizard."

Duffy looks around and shouts with joy!

"Look at my friends. We come in all different shapes, sizes, and colors, but that doesn't matter. We are really all alike. We are all beautiful. Everyone can be friends!"

"Will you be my friend too?"

Author's Note...

Why did I want everyone to meet my dog
Duffy? Because wrapped up in that little
furry body is a wise teacher with a very
big heart. Even though this book does
not have many pages or many words, the
lesson that this little pug teaches is
profound—everyone can be friends!

Connect with Duffy!

Email Duffy: duffythepugbooks@gmail.com   He would love to chat with you!

Visit Duffy on the web at: www.duffyandfriends.com and www.duffynmates.uk.

Continue the Learning

What do you remember about Duffy and his friends?

1. How many animals did Duffy meet? Count the numbers out loud.
2. Choose one animal, and tell why you would like to be friends with it.
3. What do you like about Duffy?
4. Draw a picture of Duffy playing with one of his new friends.
5. Name one of your friends. Why do you like him or her? Draw a picture of you and your friend. What makes someone a good friend? Why are friends important?
6. What was the main idea of the story?
7. What did you learn about making friends?

Say out loud each of the following words:

- Bucket
- Wild
- Pasture
- Trough
- Slide
- Wiggle

Made in the USA
Lexington, KY
12 December 2016